Every So Ofte
ZEBRA Has Spots

written by
Lauren Grabois Fischer

pictures by
Devin Hunt

The Be Books

www.TheBEbooks.com

Dedication Page

This book is dedicated to everyone!

Our differences are what make us each so beautiful.

Go out into the world and be proud of being YOU!

Thank you to my family for giving me the confidence and
courage to share my words with the world.
Thank you for always being supportive
and reading my endless amounts of poetry and stories.
I am blessed and grateful to have you in my life. To Isaac, Mollie,
Max, Joey, Naomi, Sophie, Hailey and Jessie... Be you...Always!

To my loyal readers,
thank you for becoming part of my family.

What if...

A zebra had spots

What if...

A pig loved to take baths

What if...

A flamingo ate plums instead of shrimp

What if...

What if...

A bat loved the sunshine

What if...

An octopus loved getting pedicures

What if...

A bear loved the winter

A frog said, "Meee-ooow"

What if...

A peacock had no feathers at all

What if...

What if...

A Turtle could run marathons

What if...

A skunk sprayed flowery perfume

What if...

A bee left kisses instead of stings

What a fun and exciting

world it would be!

Inspiration & Discussion

Dear Parents and Educators,

   "Every So Often A Zebra Has Spots" is a book that is meant to open our eyes to see that our world is a beautiful place because WE are ALL different. Each of our differences are special, and we should be proud of who we are. The animals in this book represent different ways that people may be different than another person. Whether we speak a different language, have different hair, or like different things... what TRULY MATTERS is what lies within us and how we treat others and ourselves. Let's work together to make this world a better place.

   On the following pages, you will find discussion questions that can guide a conversation in your home or classroom. These pages are to inspire you and your child/student(s) to think more deeply and ask the right questions. I hope that you can find meaningful conversations and enjoy each other's responses.

   With love and gratitude,

   Lauren Grabois Fischer

- How would the world be different if we saw our differences as a positive thing instead of a negative thing?

- What does kindness look like?

- What does acceptance look like? Draw a picture and share it with a friend.

- What are ways to include others? How can we make someone feel like they are important and part of the group?

- What are some ways that you can make a difference in this world?
  Age does not matter when it comes to leaving a positive imprint on our world. What can you do to make this world a better place?

- What do you think the purple flamingo represents? Does the color of our skin really define us? Does it matter if we are "pink" or "purple"? Does it matter if our skin is dark or light? Is what we have on the inside or outside more important?

- What does the pig that likes to take baths represent to you? If all of your friends are participating in one activity, does that mean that you too have to participate? Is it okay to find your own way and to find something that you enjoy? Is it okay to create your own path and be a leader instead of a follower?

- The frog in this book says, "Meee-ooow." What does a frog really say? Does the language that we speak define who we are? We each come from different parts of the world. We speak different languages based on where we grew up and where our family comes from. Speaking many languages is a gift. Learning a new language is a beautiful thing. Let's embrace the different cultures around us and learn from each other instead of being afraid of what we do not understand and know. Let's accept each other as we are. Everyone understands the language of love and kindness. We all understand what a smile and kind handshake represents. Be welcoming and kind to everyone. We all deserve it.

- The peacock that had no feathers is still beautiful. Does the color or texture of our hair define who we are? How can we be accepting of others that look different than us? Is it okay to have friends that are different than you?

- What do you think the cow that gave us lemonade instead of milk represents? Many of us have expectations put on us or we put on ourselves. There is no one way that is right. What if we do not fit the mold of what is expected of us? Does that make us undeserving of love? No! Every person deserves love and respect. Listen to your inner voice, and talk to people that you trust in your life. You need to be true to yourself always. Have trust in the process and find positive people to surround you. Be proud of what makes you, YOU.

Activity Pages

- Draw a picture of an animal that is different than it "should be". Create your own fun character that could be a part of this book.

- Name five things that you can do to include a student in your class that is feeling left out.

- Look in the mirror and name five things that you love about yourself.

1. _____

2. _____

3. _____

4. _____

5. _____

- Find a friend or family member, and tell them three things that you appreciate about them.

- Make sure that you smile at everyone that you can today. Be the reason why someone comes home happy at the end of the day.

- Fold a sheet of paper in half. Unfold it and draw two small vertical lines in the middle of the page on the fold. This will be the neck of an animal or person. Find a partner and agree to either draw the head or the body of a creature that you will create together. Cover your eyes as they draw and then switch turns. If they drew the head, they should hand you the paper with the bottom of the page empty and facing up. Draw the body of the creature and then together open the page. You will get a good laugh out of seeing the creature that you created together.

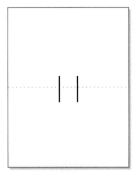

Author's Note

I am so thankful for you! Thank you for taking the time to read,
"Every So Often A Zebra Has Spots". I hope that you are feeling inspired.
You have an amazing power within to heal the world. Use your power to be kind
to others and be accepting of people from all backgrounds. Welcome that new
student in school; include a child getting left out on the playground; hold a door
open for someone; share a toy that you have with a friend; help someone with
their homework; read a book with your sibling...I bet that you can think of a
hundred ways to include someone. Let's work together to make this world a
more kind, more accepting, more respectful, more beautiful place!
And remember... BE YOU... ALWAYS.

With love and gratitude,

Lauren Grabois Fischer

Made in the USA
Las Vegas, NV
16 December 2020